GIANT
10-in-1
COLLECTION

READY READERS

STAGE 1 • PRESCHOOL-GRADE 1

A Bright Idea

Modern Publishing
A Division of Unisystems, Inc.
New York, New York 10022

Dear Parents,

Children learn to read in stages, and all children develop reading skills at different ages. **Ready Readers**™ were created to promote children's interest in reading and to increase their reading skills. **Ready Readers**™ stories are written on two levels to accommodate children ranging in age from three through eight. These stages are meant to be used only as a guide.

Stage 1: Preschool–Grade 1
Stage 1 stories are written in very short, simple sentences with large type. They are perfect for children who are getting ready to read or are just becoming familiar with reading on their own.

Stage 2: Grades 1–3
Stage 2 stories have longer sentences and are a bit more complex. They are suitable for children who are able to read but still may need help.

All the **Ready Readers**™ stories tell fun, easy-to-follow tales and are colorfully illustrated. Reading will be exciting, and soon your child will not only be ready, but eager to read.

Copyright © 1997, 1998 Modern Publishing, Inc.
A Division of Unisystems, Inc.
New York, NY 10022

™ Ready Readers is a trademark owned by Modern Publishing,
a division of Unisystems, Inc.
All rights reserved.

® Honey Bear is a trademark owned by Honey Bear Productions, Inc.,
and is registered in the U.S. Patent and Trademark Office.

All Rights Reserved.

No part of this book may reproduced or copied in any format
without written permission from the publisher.

Printed in the U.S.A.

Book UPC#: 11801
Series UPC#: 11800

2 4 6 8 10 9 7 5 3

Contents

Tommy Stays Up Late

Written by Eugene Bradley Coco
Illustrated by Robert Sabuda

Tommy had a busy day.

He went to school.

He played in the park.

He did his homework,

and he cleaned up his room.

Now it was time to go to sleep.

But Tommy was not tired.

He decided to stay up late
and watch the sun rise.

Tommy took his pillow.

He took his blanket,

and he took his favorite bear.

Tommy even took his flashlight.

Then Tommy put his chair
by the window.

He looked at the sky.

It was very dark.

He looked at the stars.
They were very bright.

He looked at the moon.

It was very big.

Soon Tommy started to get tired.

He rubbed his eyes.

Tommy let out a great big yawn.

"I must stay up," thought Tommy.
"The sun will rise soon."

But Tommy fell asleep.

Suddenly, Tommy heard
his mother calling.

"Wake up, Tommy," she said.

Tommy opened his eyes.

It was morning but it was
still dark outside.

The sun had waited for Tommy.

Walter
and the Tugboat

Written by Eugene Bradley Coco
Illustrated by Edward Heck

This is Walter the whale.

Walter lives in the deep, blue sea.

Walter likes to do many things.

He likes to splash in the waves
and spout water high in the sky.

He likes to play tag
with his friends.

But most of all,

Walter likes to watch tugboats

pull ships through the sea.

41

Big ships.

Little ships.

Sometimes the tugboats

pull two or three ships.

Here comes a tugboat now.

Walter waves his tail
as it passes by.

Captain Jim waves back.

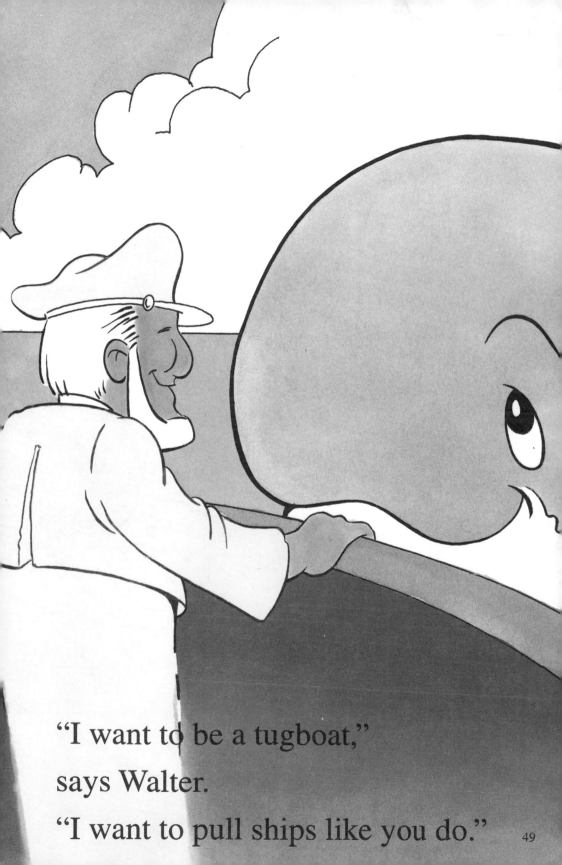

"I want to be a tugboat,"
says Walter.

"I want to pull ships like you do." 49

"You can't be a tugboat,"
laughs Captain Jim.
"You are a whale."

One day Walter sees Captain Jim's tugboat far out at sea. Something is wrong.

Captain Jim's tugboat
is not tugging.

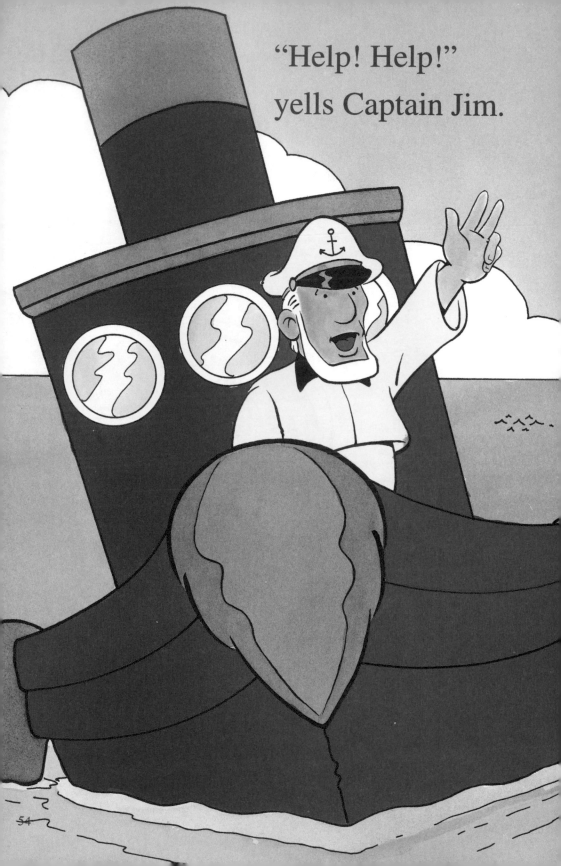

Walter swims out to the tugboat
as fast as he can.

"My tugboat is not big enough
to pull this ship,"
says Captain Jim.

Walter puts the rope in his mouth
and, with all of his might,

pulls the ship to safety.

"Thank you, Walter," says Captain Jim.

"I guess you can be a tugboat
after all."

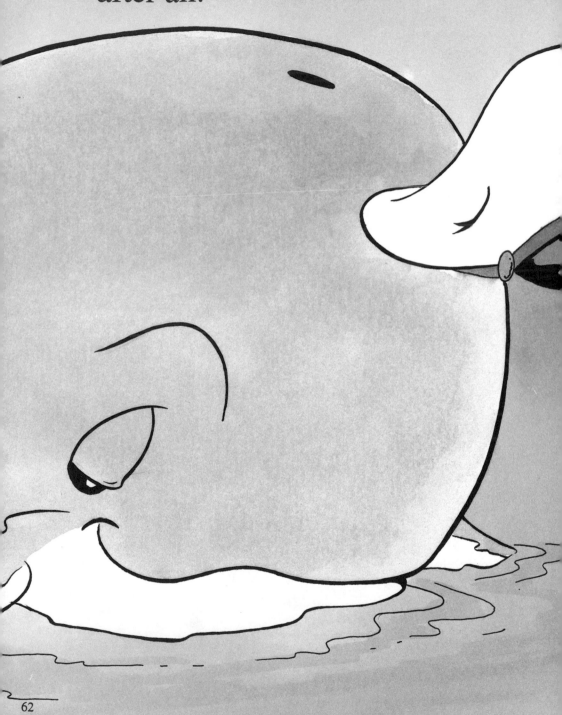

Walter smiles.

He is happy.

Now Walter is a tugboat, too.

GOLDIE'S
NEW DOGHOUSE

Written by Agatha Brown
Illustrated by Vernon McKissack

Sandy Beaver loves his
new puppy, Goldie.

He wanted to build a doghouse for Goldie.

Toni Toucan is Sandy's friend.
"I want to help," Toni said.

71

Pat the Pony is also
Sandy's friend.
"I want to help," Pat said.

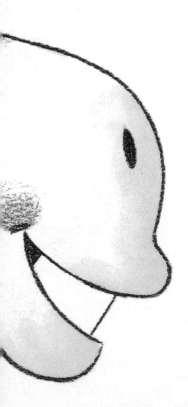

"And so do I," said
Ellie Elephant.

"Let's make a picture of what the doghouse should look like," Sandy said.

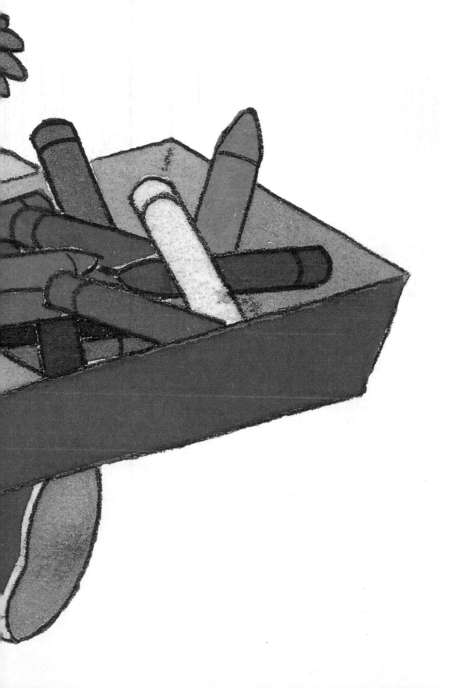

The four friends were very busy.

Everyone liked Sandy's drawing
the best.
"Now it is time to get the wood,"
Sandy said, "We need...

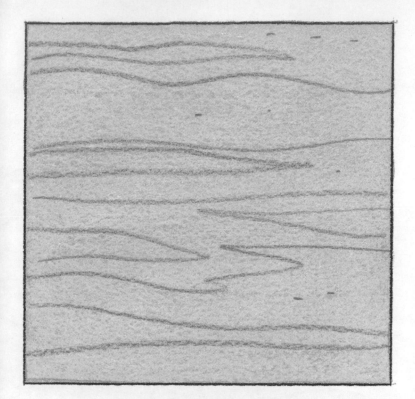

a square,

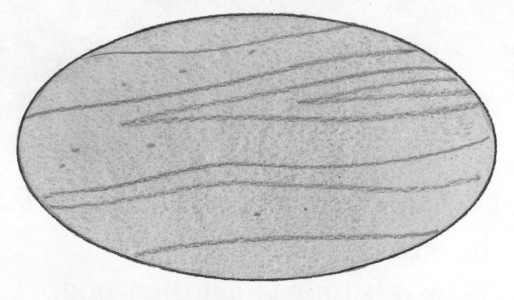

an oval,

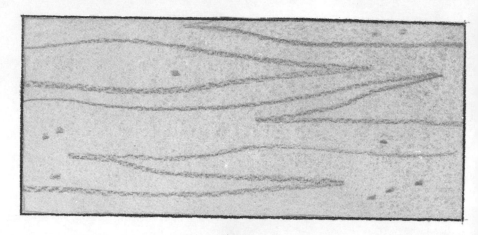

a rectangle,

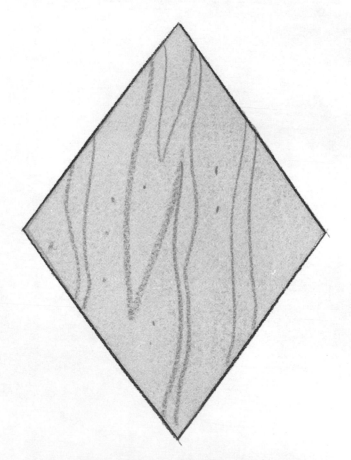

and a diamond.

We need a triangle, a crescent,

a circle and a star."

Ellie cut out a square
and an oval.

Pat cut out a diamond
and a rectangle.

Toni, Ellie, and Pat cut out all
the other shapes. Then BANG!
BANG! BANG! Sandy built the
doghouse.

Soon he called his friends to see Goldie's doghouse.

"It looks good," Toni said.

"It looks great," Pat said.

"It looks grand," Ellie said.

And Goldie loved it very much!

A BRIGHT IDEA

Written by Andrea Bear
Illustrated by Jennifer Parsons

It was time for bed.

Bear pulled down the shade.

Mouse plugged in her night light.

"Oh no!" Mouse said,
"My night light will not work.
I can't fall asleep without it."

"We can help you fall asleep,"
Bunny and Kitty said.

"Let's dance," Puppy said
and turned on the radio,
"That will make you tired."

The friends danced.
But, they did not get tired.

"Now I am hungry," Mouse said.

Bear served cookies and milk.
"Food will make you tired,"
he said.

"This is a great snack," Mouse said,
"But I am not tired."

"Bedtime stories will make Mouse
tired," Bunny and Puppy agreed.

"I will read a ghost story,"
Bunny said.

Bunny fell asleep after his story.
But everyone else was too scared
to sleep.

So Mouse read a funny story.

It was getting very late.
Everyone agreed that they should
try to sleep.

"I will
sleep in the
den with the light on,"
Mouse said, "You can sleep in
here with the light off."

Mouse walked alone down the hall.

She kept the light on, but still
could not sleep.

Mouse counted sheep.

She thought about
floating on a cloud.
Nothing helped.

Then the door opened.

"We missed you," Puppy said, "So
we thought of an idea."

Bear tied a flashlight to the door
near Mouse's bed.

"Thank you," Mouse said,
"Now we can get some sleep."

And that's what everyone did.

WHEN THE BLUEBIRD SINGS

Written by Donna Taylor
Illustrated by Edward Heck

I wake up
in the morning
when the bluebird sings.

"Good morning," I say to the
big brown squirrel.

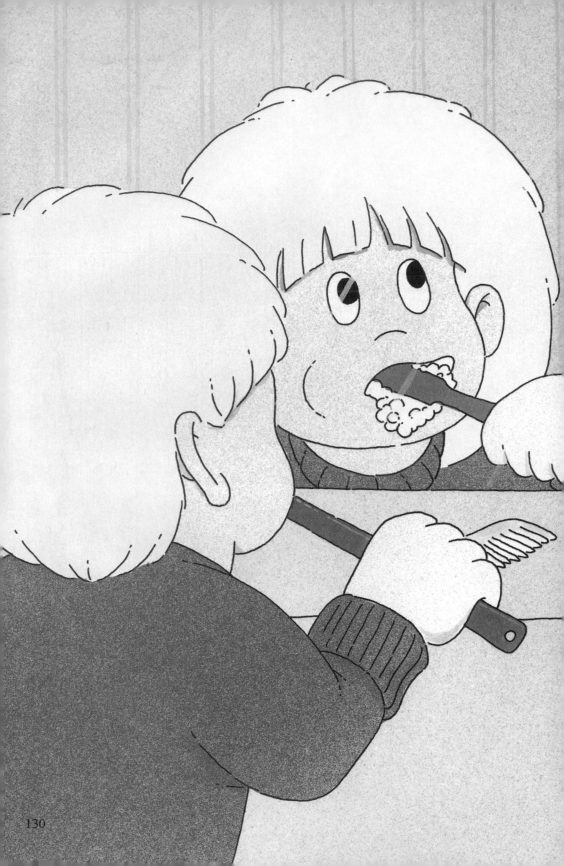

I brush my teeth.

I get dressed.

I eat my breakfast.

I go out to play.

I fly my airplane

and play ball.

Soon it's time for lunch!

What a big sandwich!

Gramps takes me to the store
in the afternoon.

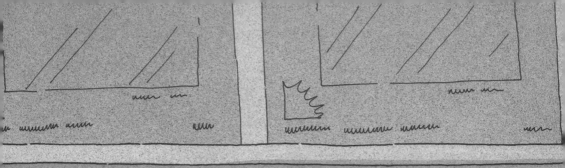

I pay the cashier all by myself.

Gramps reads me a story,
while the red bird listens
in the afternoon.

Before I know it,
it's time for dinner,
a bath, and time to brush my
teeth again!

I get into bed...

...and fall asleep...

...until morning,
when the bluebird sings.

Freckles Sneaks Out

Written by Eugene Bradley Coco
Illustrated by Susan Marino

Meet Freckles.

He is a brown cat with black spots.

He lives in a big house
with many rooms…

...and many people.

But today,

Freckles is all alone in the big house.

There is no one in the attic.

There is no one in the den.

What is Freckles to do?

"Maybe I'll go outside,"
thinks Freckles.
Outside there are
many things to do.

First, Freckles slides on the grass.

Then he rolls around in a big ball.

Next he runs to the lake.

Splish! Splash!
Freckles swims.
What fun!

Now Freckles is off to the park.

He slides down the slide.

He swings on the swings.

He monkeys around
on the monkey bars.

Suddenly, Freckles is hungry.
"It must be lunchtime,"
he thinks.

Maybe someone is back
in the big house.
Freckles runs all the way home.

Lunch is waiting for him.

Everyone is waiting for him.

They are happy to see Freckles.

Freckles is happy to see them.

Everyone has lunch.

Freckles does, too.

Freckles is happy.

He had fun outside.

Now he's ready for inside fun!

Mom's Day Off

Written by Eugene Bradley Coco
Illustrated by Colette Van Mierlo

Our mom works hard.

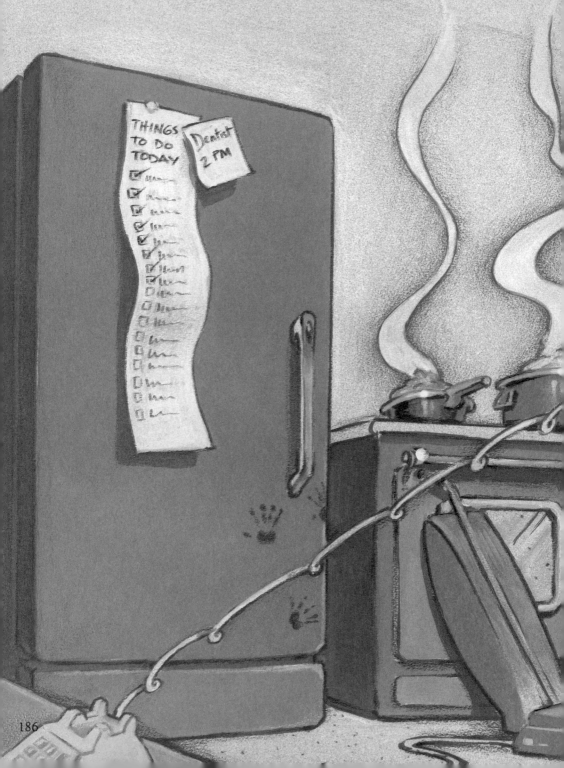

She cooks.

She cleans.

She sews our clothes
when they rip.

She takes care of us
when we're sick.

She even helps with
our homework.

Today Mom looks tired.

"Take the day off,"
we tell her.

First, we start breakfast.

"Oh, no! Watch the eggs!"

I shout.

Mom helps us clean up.

Next we straighten up the den.

Sally starts to sweep.

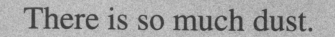

There is so much dust.

Mom helps us clear the dust.

Soon it's time for Ginger's bath.
I turn on the water.

Sally gets Ginger.

The tub is almost full.

"Wait! The faucet is stuck!"

I scream.

Here comes Mom.

The laundry is next.

We put the clothes in the
machine and add soap.
Sally turns on the washer.

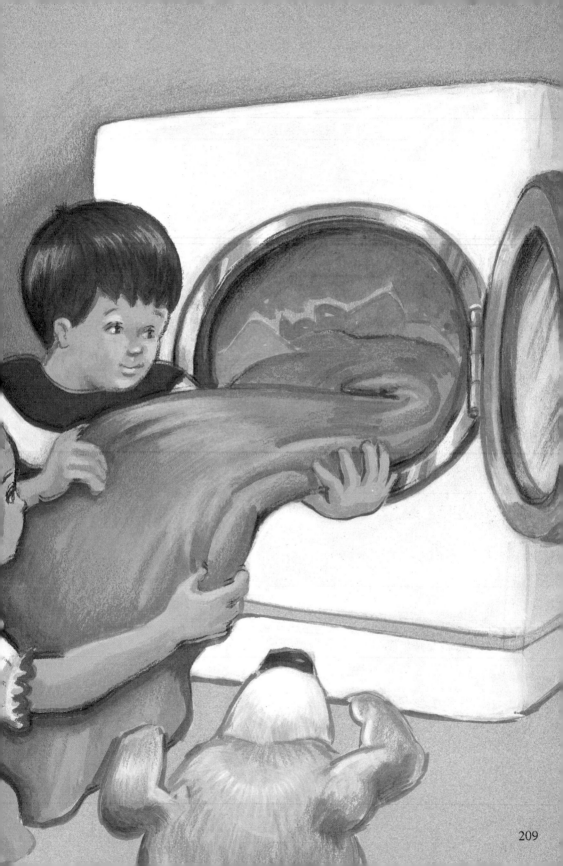

Oops!

The door isn't closed.

"Mom!" we yell.
Mom helps us pick up
the clothes.

Being in charge is hard work.
"Why don't you take the
rest of the day off?"
says Mom.

Thanks, Mom.

Peter's Present

Written by Lisa deMauro
Illustrated by Janice Castiglione

"Today is Emma's birthday. I forgot to buy her a present," Peter said.

"I must tell her that I am sorry."

Peter put on his red hat and
started for Emma's house.

A bird flew by along the way.

Then Peter saw a blue feather.

He picked it up.
"What should I do with this?
I know!" he said.

He put it on his hat.

Peter walked along until...

...he saw a yellow ribbon.

He picked it up.
"What should I do with this?"

"I know!" he said.
He put it on his hat.

Peter walked some more until...

...he saw orange flowers.

He picked some.
"What should I do with these?
I know!" he said.

He put them on his hat.

Peter walked and walked until
he saw a kite with a purple tail.
Peter pulled...

...and down came the kite tail.
"What should I do with this?
I know!" he said.
He tied the tail on his hat.

It started to rain.

Peter ran into the park.

Peter saw Kate.
She had a bag of green grapes.

"Take some," Kate said.
"Thank you," Peter said

He ate a few grapes.
"What should I do with the rest?" 237

"I know!" Peter said.

Then the rain stopped.

Peter ran to Emma's house.

Emma opened the door.
She looked at the sky.

"What a pretty rainbow and
what a nice hat," she said.

"It's a rainbow hat!" Peter said,
"I made it just for you."

"Happy Birthday, Emma!"

SAM AND PEPPER'S
TREE HOUSE

Written by Eugene Bradley Coco
Illustrated by Linda Blassingame

One day, Sam and Pepper
went for a walk in the woods.

They saw many trees,
with many branches.

Pepper jumped up on one
of the branches.

Sam climbed up to get him.
Then they both sat down
on the branch.

From up high, Sam and Pepper
could see far, far away.
They saw blue lakes
and green hills.

They even felt close to the clouds.

Sam liked sitting in the tree.

So did Pepper.

Sam had an idea.
She told Pepper.

"Woof! Woof!" Pepper barked.

Sam knew it was a good idea.
They were going to build
a tree house.

Sam got the wood.

Pepper fetched the rope.

Pepper got tangled in the rope.

Sam laughed.

Pepper laughed, too.

Then Sam got the nails,
a hammer, a saw,
some paint, and a brush.

Sam sawed the wood very carefully.
Pepper helped paint the sign—
he didn't need a brush!

"Sam and Pepper's Tree House" it read.

Sam nailed the last board in place.

The tree house was done.

Sam and Pepper climbed
into their tree house…

...and smiled.

If I Had A Hippo

Written and Illustrated by J. Ellen Dolce

If I had a hippo, I'd name it Pippo.

If I had a poodle,
I'd name it Noodle.

If I had a shark,
I'd name it Clark.

If I had a whale,
I'd name it McHale.

If I had a boa, I'd name it Noah.

If I had a bunny,
I'd name it Sunny.

If I had a sheep,
I'd name it Bo-Peep.

If I had a dragon,
I'd name it Flagon.

If I had a parrot,
I'd name it Garrot.

If I had a lizard,
I'd name it Wizard.

If I had a clam, I'd name it Sam.

If I had a squid,
I'd name it Sid.

If I had a pony,
I'd name it Baloney.

Well, I don't have
a hippo
or a poodle
or a shark
or a whale
or a boa
or a bunny
or a sheep
or a dragon
or a parrot
or a lizard
or a clam
or a squid
or a pony...

But I have a turtle,
and I named him...
Fred!